Dear Parents:

Congratulations! Your child is taking the first steps on an exciting journey. The destination? Independent reading!

STEP INTO READING® will help your child get there. The program offers five steps to reading success. Each step includes fun stories and colorful art or photographs. In addition to original fiction and books with favorite characters, there are Step into Reading Non-Fiction Readers, Phonics Readers and Boxed Sets, Sticker Readers, and Comic Readers—a complete literacy program with something to interest every child.

Learning to Read, Step by Step!

Ready to Read   Preschool–Kindergarten
• big type and easy words • rhyme and rhythm • picture clues
For children who know the alphabet and are eager to begin reading.

Reading with Help   Preschool–Grade 1
• basic vocabulary • short sentences • simple stories
For children who recognize familiar words and sound out new words with help.

Reading on Your Own   Grades 1–3
• engaging characters • easy-to-follow plots • popular topics
For children who are ready to read on their own.

Reading Paragraphs   Grades 2–3
• challenging vocabulary • short paragraphs • exciting stories
For newly independent readers who read simple sentences with confidence.

Ready for Chapters   Grades 2–4
• chapters • longer paragraphs • full-color art
For children who want to take the plunge into chapter books but still like colorful pictures.

STEP INTO READING® is designed to give every child a successful reading experience. The grade levels are only guides; children will progress through the steps at their own speed, developing confidence in their reading.

Remember, a lifetime love of reading starts with a single step!

Visit us on the Web!
StepIntoReading.com
randomhouse.com/kids

Educators and librarians, for a variety of teaching tools, visit us at RHTeachersLibrarians.com

ISBN 978-0-7364-3198-9 (trade) — ISBN 978-0-7364-8161-8 (lib. bdg.) —
ISBN 978-0-7364-3199-6 (ebook)

Printed in the United States of America   10 9 8 7 6 5 4 3 2 1

Disney·PIXAR

MONSTERS

HAPPY BIRTHDAY, MIKE!

WITHDRAWN

Adapted by Jennifer Liberts Weinberg

Based on an original story by Julie Sternberg

Illustrated by the Disney Storybook Art Team

Random House 🏠 New York

Mike and Sulley
are eating pizza.

Mike says it is
almost his birthday!
Sulley wants
to make Mike's day
extra special.

Sulley is very busy
at work.
He does not know
what to do
for Mike's birthday!

Sulley visits Boo.

He tells her

it is Mike's birthday.

Boo has a great idea!
She shows Sulley
a picture.

It is a picture
of her birthday party!
Sulley wants to have
a party for Mike.

Sulley asks his friends
for help.
They will all
plan the party.

Then they will surprise Mike!

Smitty and Needleman
gather wiggly worms
to make Mike
a mud cake!

Celia buys a
super stinky gift
for Mike!

George finds
the perfect piñata!

Pin the Forked Tail on the Monster

18

Sulley shops

for party games.

George hangs
the piñata.

Another friend
brings balloons!

Soon all Mike's
friends arrive.
They are ready
to have fun!

Chalooby carries
the punch.
Celia is excited
to play pin the tail
on the monster!
They hear something.
It must be Mike!

Mike opens the door.

He is so surprised!

He dives
into some slime!
Mike is so happy
his friends
threw him a party!

Time for snacks . . .

. . . and a yummy
birthday cake!

Birthday,
IKE!

Mike loves
his party!

Sulley is happy.
Mike had the best
birthday ever!